The Ballad of Valentine

ALISON JACKSON ♥ illustrated by TRICIA TUSA

DUTTON CHILDREN'S BOOKS • NEW YORK

Library of Congress Cataloging-in-Publication Data
Jackson, Alison.
The ballad of Valentine/by Alison Jackson; illustrated by Tricia Tusa.   p. cm.
Summary: An ardent suitor tries various means of communication, from smoke signals
to Morse code to skywriting, in order to get his message to his Valentine.
ISBN 0-525-46720-3
[1.Valentines—Fiction. 2. Stories in rhyme.] I. Tusa, Tricia, ill. II. Title.
PZ8.3.J13435 Bal 2001   [E]—dc21 2001042737

Published in the United States of America 2002 by Dutton Children's Books,
a division of Penguin Putnam Books for Young Readers
345 Hudson Street, New York, New York 10014
www.penguinputnam.com

Designed by Alyssa Morris
Printed in China • First Edition
3 5 7 9 10 8 6 4 2

For Steve, my one and only valentine
—A. J.

For my sister, Nana Banana
—T. T.

In a cabin, in a canyon,
Near a mountain laced with pine,
Lived a girl who was my sweetheart,
And her name was Valentine.

Oh my darling, oh my darling,
Oh my darling Valentine,

I have written forty letters,
But you've never read a line.

Gave the letters to a mailman
To deliver, rain or shine.

But he couldn't find your address,

So I penned this valentine.
Then I trained a homing pigeon
And attached my note with twine.

But he flew to Madagascar,
Where he dropped your valentine.

So I built a raging bonfire,
Sent a black and smoky rhyme.

But a cyclone stole the message,
And it vanished one more time.

Next I tapped a note in Morse code,
Asking you to please be mine.
But the signal hit a blizzard
As it crossed the county line.

Then I rented out a mail car
On the westward railroad line.

But the train derailed in Denver,
Leaving letters strewn behind.

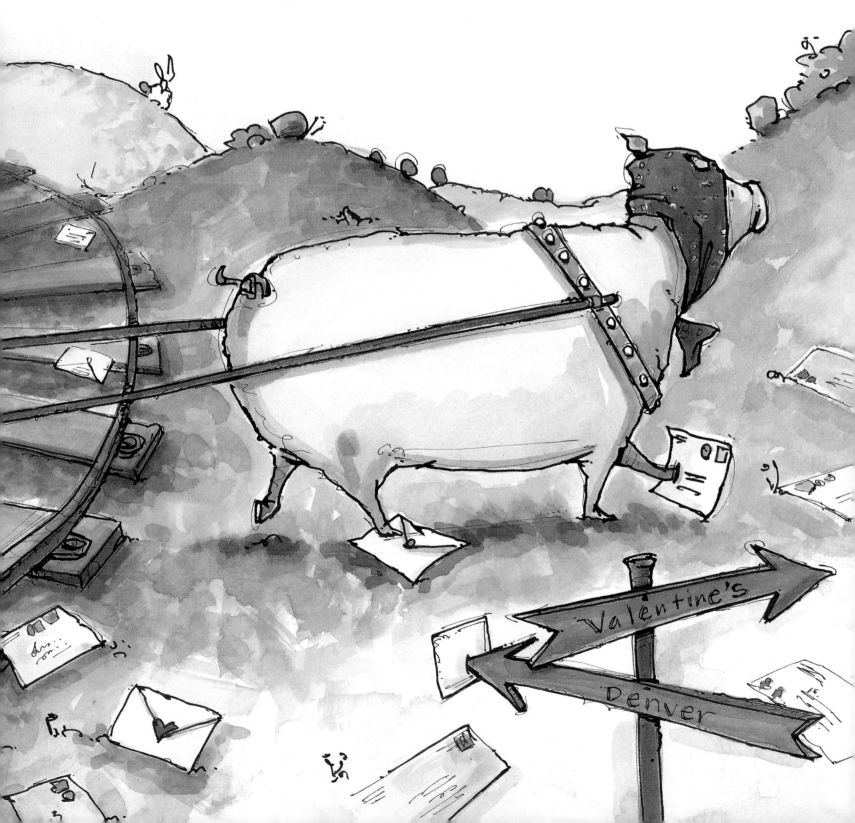

Paid a rider on a pony,
But his filly wouldn't mind.
Bucked him clear to Arizona,
Where he's now been reassigned.

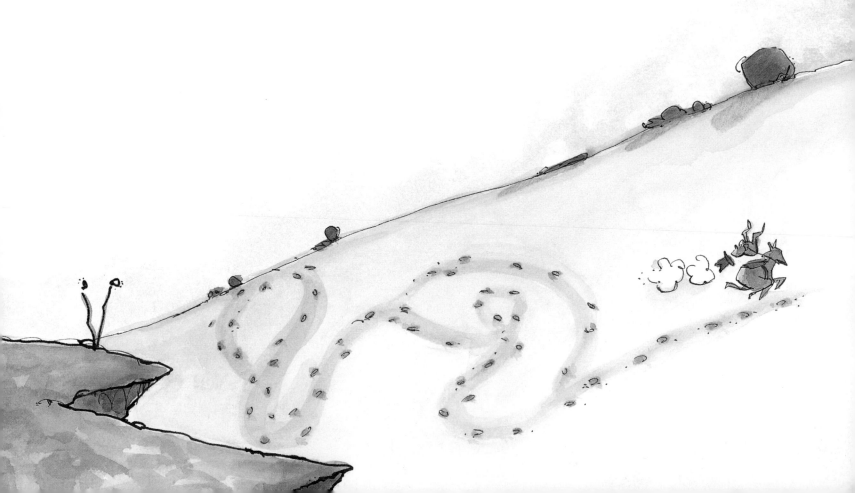

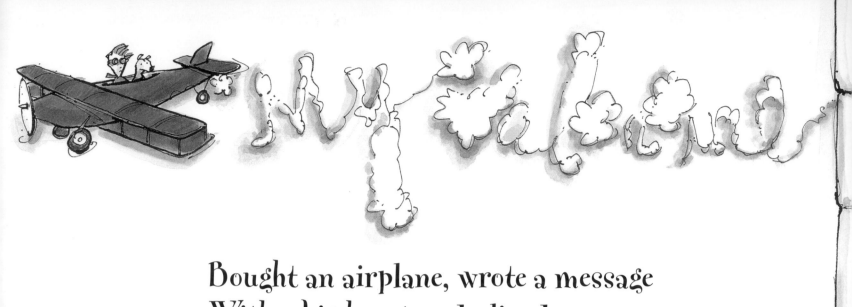

My Valentine

Bought an airplane, wrote a message
With a big heart underlined.
But the wind erased three letters,
And you're now my –al–n–ine.

Tied my message to a boulder
With a sentimental rhyme.
But it rolled down into quicksand.
Now your valentine is slime.

Well, I'm not much of a writer,
But I tried to drop a line.
If you ever get this message,

Will you be my VALENTINE?